VOLCANO OF FEAR

Written by Steve Cole

Illustrated by Miriam Serafin

RISING ★ STARS

ISBN: 9781398325586

Text © Steve Cole
Illustrations, design and layout © Hodder and Stoughton Ltd
First published in 2022 by Hodder & Stoughton Limited (for its Rising Stars imprint, part of the Hodder Education Group),
An Hachette UK Company
Carmelite House, 50 Victoria Embankment, London EC4Y 0DZ
www.risingstars-uk.com

Impression number 10 9 8 7 6 5 4 3 2 1
Year 2026 2025 2024 2023 2022

Author: Steve Cole
Series Editor: Tony Bradman
Commissioning Editor: Hamish Baxter
Illustrator: Miriam Serafin/Advocate Art
Educational Reviewer: Helen Marron
Design concept: Gary Kilpatrick
Page layouts: Rocket Design (East Anglia) Ltd
Editor: Amy Tyrer

With thanks to the schools that took part in the development of *Reading Planet* KS2, including: Ancaster CE Primary School, Ancaster; Downsway Primary School, Reading; Ferry Lane Primary School, London; Foxborough Primary School, Slough; Griffin Park Primary School, Blackburn; St Barnabas CE First & Middle School, Pershore; Tranmoor Primary School, Doncaster; and Wilton CE Primary School, Wilton.

A catalogue record for this title is available from the British Library.

Printed in the UK.

Orders: Please contact Hachette UK Distribution, Hely Hutchinson Centre, Milton Road, Didcot, Oxfordshire, OX11 7HH.

Telephone: (44) 01235 400555. Email: primary@hachette.co.uk.

Contents

The story so far

By Ana Pirelli, aged 10

My brother, Rocco, and I were accidentally picked up by a time-travelling coach from the year 3000!

The coach is owned by Time Tours, and they really live up to their name. They took us back to the year 1838 to see Queen Victoria's coronation! But the coach broke down and had to be towed back to the 31st century.

Rocco and I were left behind with a boy from the future called Ifan and Tori the tour guide. (She's a robot!)

Time Tours sent us a time pod – like a lifeboat for people lost in time. It was meant to take us through time and back to the 21st century, but we flew into some junk on the way.

We crash-landed in a city in sixth-century Mexico! We saved the people there from an enemy army, and Tori managed to fix the damage to the pod so we could escape.

Now I just hope the pod is properly repaired. If it isn't, who knows if we will ever get back home …

1 Follow that time ship!

"I still can't believe we're travelling through time!" said Ana, staring at the swirling lights through the time pod's windscreen.

Her brother, Rocco, nodded. "Who knew you could catch a ride to different times in history like they're stops on a bus route! *Ding!* Get off here for ancient Egypt!"

"Ha!" said Ifan. He came from the year 3000, so was used to time travel, but each trip still filled him with wonder. "Could that be our next stop, Tori?"

"Er, it's hard to tell," said Tori. She was pressing buttons and twisting controls, a frown on her metal face. "We took off so fast, the main computer wasn't ready. It's causing power surges in the systems."

"Can you call Time Tours?" said Rocco. "Get them to send help?"

Sparks fizzed from the control panel.

"I can't," said Tori, checking the damage. "*That* power surge just blew up our time radio!"

Suddenly, something streaked past them through the whirl of lights outside.

"What was that?" asked Ana.

"I believe it was another vessel passing by!" said Tori. "It might be a Time Tours coach. Perhaps we could use *their* radio? I'll try to follow them." She pressed more buttons and the time pod suddenly sped up and started to shake. "Whoops! That time ship is towing something big behind it. It's causing ripples and bumps in the time flow – and we're flying through them!"

"I hate time turbulence," said Ifan, looking green.

"If it's going to be a bumpy ride," said Ana, "we could turn our wonder-onesies into padded suits to protect ourselves."

The children were wearing white hooded overalls – called wonder-onesies – that could change into any costume from any time in history!

Invented in the future, they were perfect for time travellers who wanted to blend in wherever they went.

"Wonder-onesies," said Ifan, "dress us all in cotton-wool suits from the 26th century!"

The smart clothes glowed as they started to work. But then smoke began pouring from the futuristic fabric.

"What happened?" asked Ana, looking down at her scorched plastic outfit.

"Another power surge!" Tori squeaked. "I'm afraid the wonder-onesies have blown a fuse."

The shifting lights faded from the time pod's windscreen. Suddenly, there was clear, blue ocean beneath them!

"We're over the sea!" Ana realised. The time pod was dropping towards the water, but there was a sandy beach ahead of them.

"Prepare for a splash-landing!" squeaked Tori.

The time pod bounced on the waves towards the empty beach. The children clung together, rocking about as the pod slithered up the sand. It finally skidded to a stop inside a cave.

"Down and safe!" said Tori with relief. Quickly, she switched off the systems. "Right. I'll restart the main computer – it will only take a few hours. There shouldn't be any more power surges after that."

"But what about the radio?" Rocco grumbled. "We can't call anyone for help."

"And with the wonder-onesies broken, we can't fit in with the local people," said Ana. "Who *are* the local people, anyway?"

"Romans!" said Tori, looking at a screen. "We are in a small town in Italy called Oplontis. It is August 23rd in the year 79 AD."

The satellite dish on her head spun around at top speed. "Oh, my goodness! This is a very dangerous date in history," she went on.

"How come?" asked Rocco.

"You'll see," said Tori, opening the door. "Take off those broken wonder-onesies and join me outside."

Rocco and Ana were still wearing their school uniforms under their wonder-onesies. Ifan brushed down his shimmering blue jumpsuit.

"This is the only outfit I own," he said. "In my time, wonder-onesies let us pretend we have lots to wear."

"I guess that's better for the environment," said Ana.

"There's not much of the environment left in the year 3000," Ifan said sadly. "The Earth is totally polluted. It's like one big rubbish dump."

"No wonder everyone there likes coming into the past," said Rocco.

Tori beckoned to them from the mouth of the cave. She led the way across the deserted beach to a set of steps that ran up the cliff face.

They reached the top, with a good view over the town. They saw a group of fancy-looking villas and a small market square.

"So, this is Oplontis," said Ifan. "Where is the danger?"

As he spoke, the ground rumbled. A wisp of smoke curled up from a mountain on the hilly horizon.

"*There's* the danger," said Tori. "*That* volcano, to be precise," she continued, pointing to the smoky mountain. "It's Mount Vesuvius – the most deadly volcano in Europe. In 24 hours, it's going to blow – and destroy everything for miles around!"

2 A rubbish discovery

Rocco stared at the smouldering mountain with horror. "That volcano is going to blow *tomorrow*?"

Tori nodded. "When it erupts, it will blast out 1.5 million tonnes of molten rock and ash every second," she explained. "Blazing destruction will rain down all around, burying everything from nearby Pompeii to this very town."

"That's horrible," said Ana. "But what about the people we followed here? Why would anyone time-travel to a huge disaster like this on purpose?"

"Maybe they're scientists who've come to study the volcano?" Ifan suggested.

"The only way to know for sure is to find them," said Rocco. "Then, maybe we can use their time radio to call for help!"

"Let's start in the market square," Ana suggested. "We can ask if anyone's seen strangers in town."

"I shall go looking elsewhere," said Tori. "I think a silver robot might draw too much attention in a Roman market! But don't worry, my brain-to-voice translation will still work for you, so you can talk to the people here."

The children walked along the path to the market in bright sunshine. The salty sea air gave way to the smell of flowers, herbs and fruit. But Ana's eyes kept being drawn to the dark shadow of the looming volcano.

Tomorrow, it erupts, she thought. *And nobody living here knows it!*

The market was noisy. Sellers shouted about their goods – everything from meat and fish to tools and blankets – trying to attract customers.

"We really stand out in these clothes," said Ifan.

"So does she," said Rocco, pointing. "Look over there."

Ana could hardly believe her eyes as she saw a woman standing beside a market stall dressed in a shimmering blue jumpsuit, like Ifan's!

The sleeves were cut off and it looked dirty in places, but it was definitely the same special material.

"Another time traveller?" Ifan said. "Perhaps she's from that ship we followed here."

"Hi!" called Rocco, walking up to her. "Can we use your time radio?"

"My *what*?" The woman looked confused.

"Aren't you from the future, then?" asked Ana.

"I'm from Rome," said the woman proudly.
"I'm Camilla."

"Where did you find that outfit, Camilla?" Ana asked.

"In the pit," said Camilla. "Your clothes are amazing, by the way. Are they from the pit, too?"

"Er, no," said Rocco quickly. "What pit?"

"It's on the edge of town. Weird stuff appears there." Camilla pulled a face. "Most of it is smelly and horrible, but you get some good things, too. Take this incredible vase for instance. It's like glass, but you can bend it!"

From behind the stall, she produced what looked like an empty squash bottle. "Isn't that brilliant?"

"Plastic!" Rocco whispered.

"Plastic wasn't invented until the 20th century," said Ifan. "It shouldn't be here."

"And look at this amazing hat!" Camilla showed them a dented plastic helmet with wires sticking out of it. She put it on her head. "You'll be the envy of everyone in a hat like this."

"That's a lesson zapper," said Ifan. He turned to Rocco and Ana and lowered his voice. "Robot teachers wear them in the year 3000 – they zap school lessons straight into pupils' heads. But that one looks broken."

"Broken?" Camilla overheard. "I think you mean *stylish*."

Ana turned back to Camilla. "Where can we find this pit?"

"It's near the empty villa on the hill," said Camilla, pointing behind her. "But be careful. People say they've seen ghosts around the pit. One glows red and one glows blue. Most people don't dare go near." She grinned. "But I do, because whenever the ghosts are seen, new treasures appear in the pit! And that means new things for me to sell."

With a wave to Camilla, the children moved away.

"A pit full of stuff that doesn't belong in this time ..." said Rocco thoughtfully. "We'd better check it out."

"Someone is checking *us* out," Ifan whispered. "Look across the market square."

Sure enough, Rocco and Ana noticed a grey-haired man staring their way, dressed in plain white robes. He called a shorter man with an eyepatch over to him, and they began to talk.

"I don't like the look of them," said Ana. "Come on, let's get out of here."

They left the market and reached a quieter street. "Which way to the pit now?" wondered Ifan.

Rocco sniffed – and caught a whiff of old rubbish. "I think we can probably follow our noses!"

As they walked out of Oplontis, the paved road became little more than a dirt track leading up a hill. At the top was a once-grand villa. The lower part of the building was crumbling, but the third floor seemed newly built. Some of the white stone columns at the front had cracked, and some had even collapsed. The garden was overgrown.

"I guess that's the empty villa on the hill Camilla told us about," said Rocco. "The pit must be near here."

"It is!" said a familiar, squeaky voice beside them. Tori popped out from behind a large, white boulder.

"Tori!" Ana was glad to see the robot. "Did you find anything?"

"I don't know where the other time travellers are, but I've seen what they have left behind," Tori said. "Quickly, come with me."

They followed Tori down a winding track. The smell of rubbish got steadily worse, filling their nostrils.

As they rounded a corner, Ana gasped. Ahead of them was a vast sea of plastic junk and electronic rubbish, stretching out as far as the eye could see.

"This junk doesn't belong in Roman times," said Ifan. "It's from the future!"

Rocco couldn't believe what he was seeing. The pit was packed with machine parts, plastic bags and bottles, mouldy food and worn-out clothes.

"There's got to be a trillion tons of trash here!" Ifan cried. "Do you think the time travellers we followed have been bringing it back from the future and dumping it in this pit?"

"But why would they do that?" said Ana.

"It's dreadful!" Tori squawked. "Ancient Romans shouldn't be let near this stuff."

Rocco nodded. "Imagine if Ifan's lesson zapper thing started working. Camilla would learn things from 3000 years in the future."

"And she could teach others," Tori agreed. "They could build machines out of this junk and change the ancient world. Things like this are forbidden by every time-travel law ..."

"Maybe the time travellers we followed are investigating, too?" Ifan suggested. He pointed to the crumbling villa on top of the hill. "Maybe we'll see their ship from up there?"

"Good idea," Ana agreed.

Together, the four friends walked up the path towards the ruined villa. Everything was quiet. Rocco felt a tingle of fear travel down his spine. *What if there really were ghosts around here?* he thought.

Ana tried the front door, but it was locked. Tori pushed with her robotic strength. There was the sound of wood splintering, and then a bolt jangled to the floor. The door creaked open.

"Hello?" called Rocco nervously. No one answered.

They stepped into a dusty hallway.

"Look," said Ifan. "Footprints."

The footprints led them into an overgrown courtyard. Couches and chairs stood here and there, half-covered in weeds. There were steps leading to the first floor, but the footprints continued into a garden.

"They lead up to that old statue," said Ifan.

Rocco looked at the statue – it was an athlete. Moss was growing all over the old stone – apart from on the athlete's right arm, which looked much cleaner. Rocco touched the arm ... and it moved!

"Hey, look at this," he said. "I think this is a secret lever!"

Ana joined Rocco and twisted the statue's arm upwards. It made a grating, mechanical noise, and the ivy covering the garden was pulled by long wires to one side of the courtyard.

The ivy had been hiding a vast hole in the solid rock that stretched down into shadows.

Two strange machines had been left near the top. One stood on a platform: it looked like a red, metal digger with mechanical jaws. The other was blue, floating in a pool of water, like a submarine, with huge magnets sticking out from it.

"The red machine is a mega-digger," said Tori. "It cuts through rock as easily as you can bite through mashed potato. The blue one is a magna-drag. It moves anything metal with its super-strong magnets."

"Camilla said that people had seen red and blue ghosts," Ana recalled. "Maybe they really saw the mega-digger and the magna-drag?"

"I wonder what else is hidden away down here?" Tori's eyes glowed into torch beams as she stared into the hole, scanning the darkness. Some way below, huge, pink, metal containers gleamed in the light.

"Trash tins," said Ifan. "In the 30th century, they float about collecting people's rubbish. They squash it all inside, then go to the dump and spit everything out."

Tori switched off her torch beams and looked at the children. "I think I should go down there and investigate further," she said. "If we do manage to call for help, I must know all the facts. Wait for me here."

"Why can't we come with you?" said Ana.

"Because you cannot jump as splendidly as a robot!" said Tori.

As if to show them what she meant, she leaped five metres down into the darkness and landed with a wobble on a trash tin.

"Now, pull the statue's arm," she called up. "We cannot risk any ancient Romans learning of modern machines! I'll call to you when I'm back."

"All right," Rocco hissed down to her. "Be careful."

Ifan twisted the stone athlete's arm and the ivy stretched across to hide the underground base once more.

Ifan led the way back into the half-covered courtyard. Suddenly, the ground rumbled beneath their feet. "That must be the volcano!" said Ana, staggering across the floor. A large slab of plaster shook down from a wall. It exploded over the floor in a cloud of white dust, and the children coughed, blinded.

"I thought I saw people heading here," came a deep voice from the hall in front of them. "This is a dangerous place to be."

Rocco gulped and clutched at Ana's arm. "The other time travellers," he hissed. "They've found us!"

But as the dust cleared, they saw a familiar man in white robes standing in the doorway.

"We saw you in the market," Ana said, wary of the stranger. "Why are you here?"

The man smiled. "My name is Marcus Cornelius Dominus. These earthquakes are getting worse. I think you should come with me to somewhere safer."

"No thanks," said Rocco quickly, not trusting this man one bit. "We're good here."

"But you don't live in this villa, do you?" said Marcus with a sly smile. "You are trespassing."

"We know the owners," said Ifan with a shrug. "We just dropped in to see them."

"No." Marcus shook his head. "If you knew the owners like *I* do, you would know that they live in Rome. This was their holiday home. When the earthquakes here started getting worse, they decided not to return." He frowned. "I'm surprised they built a third floor on top of the old place. Perhaps they're trying to sell it."

"That's right, they are!" bluffed Rocco. "We came here to help them."

"Nonsense," said Marcus. He took a step closer. "I can tell from the way you dress and act that none of you are real Romans. And if you're from outside the Empire, that means I can sell you as slaves!"

Ana's eyes widened. "What?"

"I am a slave trader." Marcus grinned like a hungry wolf. "Many people want strong, healthy children like you to work for them. You will make me a lot of money when I sell you to the highest bidder!"

"You can't do that!" Rocco spluttered.

"I can and I will," said Marcus. "I have many other slaves locked up, and my ship is waiting in the harbour. In the morning, we will leave Oplontis and sail round the coast to Rome, ready for the big slave auction. And there's enough room to take the three of you!"

4 Danger at sea

"I'm not going to be a slave," Ifan yelled at the slave trader. "Rocco, Ana – run!" He started up the steps to the first floor. But a figure burst into sight on the balcony. It was the man with the eyepatch they'd seen back in the market.

"Ah, there you are, Cyclops!" Marcus said to the man. "Get the boy!" Cyclops grunted and grabbed Ifan.

"Leave him alone!" shouted Ana. "Come on, Rocco!" But before they could run to help Ifan, Marcus produced a heavy net from under his robes. He hurled it over Ana and Rocco, and they fell beneath its weight. Ifan broke free of Cyclops's grip. But the one-eyed man simply brought out his own net and threw it over Ifan, who fell to the ground.

"Tie them up and load them on the cart, Cyclops," said Marcus. "They're coming with us!"

In the nets, Ana, Rocco and Ifan couldn't stop Cyclops binding their wrists and ankles.

They found themselves being carried on to a wooden cart drawn by two horses.

"Make yourselves comfortable," Marcus laughed. "Come on, Cyclops, let's get to the harbour ..."

Soon the horses were clip-clopping away down the dirt track.

"Shall we call for help?" Rocco suggested.

"There's no point," said Ana. "Romans thought slavery was a good thing."

"Well, Tori is still out there," said Rocco. "We just have to hope she'll track us down."

Hours passed. The warmth of the day faded as night began to fall.

"We can't be far from Marcus's ship now," said Rocco.

"I've almost got my hands free," Ana whispered. "Yes!" Her wrists and fingers were super-sore from all the rubbing, but she quickly started on the ropes round her ankles. Finally free, she began pulling at the knots in Rocco's ropes.

"Keep going," Rocco said. "I think they're coming loose."

Once Rocco was untied, he and Ana helped Ifan. They released Ifan just as the cart slowed to a stop. The children held their breaths under the sheet as they heard Marcus and Cyclops get out. But the men didn't come for them – they moved away from the cart.

"Let's get out of here," said Rocco.

He stuck his head out from under the sheet and peeped about. A full moon shone in the sky. Its silver light glinted on the dark and shifting sea. The harbour was full of boats. Most were long and enormous, with a dozen oars on each side sticking out through portholes.

They had square sails that flapped in the breeze, like the wings of giant bats. Fires burned in metal baskets on the harbourside like smoky streetlamps. People chatted, drank and argued in the flickering light.

But as Rocco, Ana and Ifan clambered out from underneath the cover, a bearded man came up behind them.

"You poor children," the bearded man said. "Are you trying to escape?"

"Yes! We've been caught by a slave trader," Rocco whispered.

The bearded man nodded. "Come with me. Quickly." He ushered Rocco, Ana and Ifan over a wooden plank and on to a dirty ship towards a flight of slippery steps. "You can hide out below decks."

"Thank you!" said Rocco. He, Ana and Ifan ducked down into the darkness beneath the deck.

But, once there, the man pushed the children into a small space with wooden bars, like a prison cell – and slammed a door on them!

"Hey!" said Ana angrily, gripping the bars. "Don't lock us up in here!"

"You shouldn't have trusted me, slaves. I'm the captain of Marcus's ship!" He smiled smugly. "I just pulled into harbour. Thanks for saving me the bother of having to carry you off the cart!"

"And don't worry, you'll have plenty of company," came the familiar voice of Marcus through the darkness.

"I've just been rounding up my other slaves to be sold." The captain opened the barred door again and about 30 ragged men, women and children squashed in around Ana, Ifan and Rocco.

"We leave for Rome at first light," said Marcus. "By teatime tomorrow, I'll have sold the whole lot of you!"

"So much for getting away," said Ifan miserably.

Rocco sighed. "I think I preferred being tied up on the cart!"

The night passed slowly. Ana didn't sleep a wink.

As the sun rose at last, Ana watched through the bars as 24 men came down into the belly of the ship. They sat on benches and gripped their oars. The captain barked commands at the oarsmen and, as one, they began to row.

The ship shifted and rocked as it moved off through the water.

"Next stop, Rome," said Ifan grimly. "I hope we're all sold to the same owner at least."

Rocco nodded, a lump in his throat.

"Don't talk that way," Ana said. "We can't give up ..."

She trailed off as the ship began to shake. The oarsmen stared around in alarm. The enslaved people clung together, afraid.

Suddenly, there was an enormous, muffled explosion somewhere out at sea. The ship rocked wildly, and a sonic boom cracked through the sky.

"What was that?" Ifan yelled as people cried out in fear. "Was it the volcano?"

"No." Rocco peered out through a small porthole towards the coast. A stretch of sea about 100 metres away was glowing red and churning with fiery light. "I think something's blown up below the surface," he said. Then he gulped at the sight of an enormous wave rising up towards them. "And I think the blast has started a tsunami ... When it hits, it'll smash us to bits!"

5 Threat beneath the waves

Rocco tore his eyes from the huge wall of water rolling towards the ship and called to the captain and the oarsmen. "You've got to do something," he shouted. "We need to get away from that wave!"

Marcus came running down from the deck. "The sea is on fire!" he yelled. "Row faster, you fools. The ocean is wild and wants to swallow us!"

But the warnings came too late. Rocco, Ifan and Ana clung together as the slave ship rose up on the swell of the wave – and then tipped over!

"Take a deep breath!" Ana shouted. Cold seawater smashed through the sides of the ship. The timber walls broke open. The children were thrown about with their fellow captives as the ship somersaulted.

Rocco found himself falling through water in a dizzying rush. With all his strength, he swam up to the surface and gulped for air. His body ached all over and his eyes stung with salty water. He saw the ship had been battered to bits – scraps of wood floated on the water like jigsaw pieces. People held on to the driftwood or swam for shore. Marcus, Cyclops and the captain clung to the ship's mast, shivering together.

"Ana?" Rocco shouted desperately for his sister. "Ifan? Where are you?"

"Rocco, here!" Ana's voice came from behind him. She was keeping herself afloat while trying to stop Ifan sinking into the water – he was knocked out and had a red bump on his head. "Something must have hit him."

"Quickly," came a familiar, squeaky voice. "Get in."

"Tori!" Rocco and Ana cried together.

Floating on the surface, bobbing towards them, was the time pod. Tori had already opened the door.

Panting, Rocco and Ana managed to heave Ifan on board and into a seat. "I'm so pleased to see you!" said Ana. "How did you find us?"

"You know I scan the brainwaves of all my tour passengers in case they wander off and get into trouble," said Tori with a smile. "And you three are always getting into trouble!"

Ifan's eyes flickered open, and he smiled at Ana and Rocco. "What happened?" he said. "Wow, my head hurts. Where have you been, Tori?"

Tori's satellite dish spun around like she was thinking. "I have been exploring, making awful discoveries – and coming to your rescue!"

"Discoveries?" said Rocco. "Do you know what caused that explosion?"

"I will show you," said Tori grimly. "Close the door."

"No, wait. First, we must help these poor people that Marcus captured," said Ana. "They were meant to go to Rome – not drown in the sea!"

"Very well," said Tori with a nod. Carefully, she steered the time pod round to a piece of driftwood with three people clinging to it. They saw Tori's silver skin and gasped.

"Don't be scared," said Ana. "Tori is in disguise ... er, and so is her boat."

Rocco nodded. "She doesn't want Marcus Thingummy Thingummy to know who she is."

The people in the water let go of their driftwood and held on to the side of the time pod. Tori had activated handles for them to hold on to. Others came swimming over and held on as Tori slowly drove towards shore.

"What about us?" yelled Marcus as Cyclops waved for help beside him.

Rocco saw a Roman galley pushing out from the harbour. "You're lucky that a ship is coming to rescue you," he shouted. "Just don't come after these people – they're free now!"

"Right," Ana added. "And Oplontis is not a good place to be right now!"

As Tori reached the beach, their grateful passengers staggered out of the water.

"Run, all of you," Rocco urged them. "Leave Oplontis as quickly as you can."

"Thank you!" cried a boy.

"We're free!" cheered a woman. "It's a miracle!" Whooping and laughing, no longer prisoners, the rest of the people ran away across the beach.

"How long have they got to get clear?" Ana asked.

"Five hours and fifteen minutes," Tori told her. "Then, the volcano blows. Now, close the door and let's get back in the water. I have to show you what I've found."

Tori twisted some controls, and the time pod turned and sank down beneath the waves. "We don't have a minute to lose!" she said.

"Have you been able to repair the time radio?" asked Ifan. "So we can get help?"

"I'm afraid not. But at least I can help *you*," said Tori. She reached beneath her seat and pulled out a futuristic first-aid kit. It shone a warm light on Ifan's head, and his bump went down. "There. This will give you a healing sleep."

Ifan yawned and started snoring softly. Ana fastened his safety belt for him.

"I only wish I could resolve the rest of our problems so easily!" said Tori, switching on the headlights as they dived deeper.

Rocco and Ana joined her at the controls to peer out through the windscreen. Ahead of them, in the murky light, they saw dozens of mysterious metal shapes lying on the seabed. Some were sleek and small. Others were large and twisted.

"What are those things?" asked Ana.

"They are vehicles from the year 3000," said Tori. "Ultrasonic rockets, space cars, time ships ... all of them worn out or broken beyond repair. And they all have dangerous atomic engines that could pollute and poison the water."

"More nasty, old junk," Rocco muttered. "Was it one of those vehicles that exploded?"

"Yes," said Tori. "It was a crashed moon shuttle with leaking fuel rods."

Ana thought back to their last adventure, in Mexico, when their time pod had exploded. "We know how harmful fuel rods can be to the environment."

"That exploding moon shuttle might have changed history!" said Tori crossly. "If the blast had been bigger, it could have destroyed the whole harbour instead of just one ship!"

"I'm guessing whoever did this doesn't care," said Ana. "How did these wrecks get down here, under the ocean?"

"Remember the machines we found hidden at the villa?" said Tori. "I found a tunnel from there down to the seabed. Whoever's behind this must have used the mega-digger to make it."

"And I suppose they used that magna-drag thing to drag these wrecks through the tunnel," Rocco realised. "But *why*?"

"That's what we have to discover before the volcano blows," said Tori.

Suddenly, something clanged against the left side of the time pod.

Rocco jumped. "What was that? Did we hit something?"

CLANG! Now something clanged against the *right* side of the time pod.

Two metal faces slid up into view through the windows. They each had glowing circles for eyes and a black slit for a mouth. One was red with three spikes sticking up from its round head, the other was blue with a head like a cube.

"Okay, so robots definitely don't belong in ancient Rome," said Rocco. "We wanted to find whoever's been dumping the trash here – but I think they've found us!"

"Excuse me," Tori told the robots primly. "This vessel is owned by Time Tours and is for customers only. No extra passengers allowed."

The robots ignored her. The red one smashed its fist against the window. The blue one did the same. Cracks began to appear in the glass.

"They're trying to force their way inside," cried Ana. "If they break the glass, we'll drown!"

6 Race against time

"Hold on," said Tori as the robots went on beating at the time pod's windows. "I'll see if I can shake them off!"

Rocco and Ana strapped themselves in – just in time – as Tori hit the speed control. The time pod whooshed forward through the water. The robots' magnetic grip slipped, but Tori couldn't shake them loose.

"I have an idea," Ana shouted. "Tori, take us into the tunnel that leads to the villa. Perhaps we can scrape these robots off against the sides."

"Okay, here goes!" Tori turned the time pod around and jetted off through the murky water.

WHAM! Another red robot fist pounded against the side of the pod.

"Quickly, Tori," Ana urged her.

"Here's the mouth of the tunnel!" Tori said, pointing to a cave gaping in an undersea cliff. The time pod shot inside and then turned sharply upwards into a rocky shaft, flying like a yellow torpedo. They burst from the dark water, and Tori carefully steered the time pod against the stone sides of the shaft. There was a horrible grinding noise. Sparks flew. A burning smell filled the cabin.

"The robots are still holding on!" Ana cried, as a blue metal fist smashed into the window again and left more cracks.

"We must be nearly back at the villa," yelled Rocco, pointing ahead through the windscreen. "Look, the shaft is getting wider – and there are those trash tin things that sucked up all the rubbish."

Four pink trash tins were stuck to the side of the narrow shaft. Tori steered towards them – then swept away at the last moment. With two deafening *CLANGs*, the robots banged against the trash tins and were knocked free!

"You did it, Tori!" Ana cheered.

Tori whizzed past the magna-drag and mega-digger at the top of the shaft, tore through the ivy, and whooshed out into the sunlight. She landed with a bump on solid ground in front of the empty villa.

"Phew!" said Tori, opening the bashed-in door. "That was close."

"I feel like I left my stomach somewhere in the ocean," said Rocco, climbing out unsteadily after her.

"Ifan slept through the whole thing!" Ana reported. "Is the time pod okay?"

"The engines almost overloaded," said Tori. "They need to cool down before we can take off again."

"As long as they're good to go before the volcano erupts," said Ana. "Why did those robo-creeps attack us like that?"

"I can only assume they don't want us telling anyone what they're up to," said Tori.

Rocco peered down into the darkness of the giant hole. "Do you think they will come after us again?"

"Maybe. They can swim underwater and are super-tough," said Tori. "We must find their time ship quickly and use its radio to warn Time Tours about what's been happening. They will send time officers to help put things right."

Rocco nodded. "Let's start looking."

Ana pointed down the hill to some caves in the side of a cliff on the far side of the pit. "Perhaps their ship is hidden down there?" she said. "Should we wake Ifan?"

Tori shook her head. "He should sleep until his bump is better. Come on."

They hurried down the hillside. Ana and Rocco both felt tired and thirsty but knew there was no time to rest. They peered into each cave in turn. There were a few bits of rubbish blown down from the big pit, but otherwise the caves were empty. The friends kept searching, climbing several more hills and looking all about. But there was still no sign of the time ship.

"How long now until volcano o'clock?" asked Rocco.

"Less than two hours," said Tori. "Oh dear! Oh goodness! Perhaps we should give up and get back to the time pod."

"Not yet," Rocco argued. "You said it won't be ready, anyway." He paused to think. "Wait. When the Time Tours coach parked in Victorian London, it hid itself as a long caravan that wouldn't stand out. Maybe those robots have a way to hide *their* ship."

"So, it could be anything?" said Ana. "That will make it even harder to find ..." She trailed off – and then groaned. "Of course, that's it!"

"What's what?" said Rocco.

Ana pointed back up the hillside to the old villa. "The top floor on that house," she said, her eyes shining with excitement. "Marcus said he didn't know who'd built it, remember? The owners left the villa because of the earthquakes."

Tori smiled. "No one would be foolish enough to build a new floor on top of a falling-down building."

"*That* must be the robots' time ship in disguise!"

"All their other stuff is hidden at the villa," Rocco said. "It makes sense for their ride home to be there, too!"

Ana started back up the hillside towards the villa. "Let's check it out."

But, just then, a flat, buzzing voice carried from over the hill. "The owners of that time pod must be hunted down ... and dealt with!"

"Hide!" hissed Rocco. He dived for the cover of a nearby boulder, and Ana and Tori followed.

Two battered metal robots – one red, one blue – strode into sight over the brow of the hill. In their metal-clamp hands they held torch-like gadgets.

"Looks like the trash tins didn't eat them after all," Rocco whispered.

"And they have laser blasters," squeaked Tori.

Suddenly, there was a chime like a phone's ringtone. "Calling Trash-bot Alpha!"

The red robot pulled up a spike from its head, like an aerial. "Yes, Master? This is Alpha."

"Have you placed all the rubbish in position?" came a robotic squawk on the speakerphone.

"Yes, Master," said Alpha. "When Mount Vesuvius erupts, it will release more energy than 100,000 atom bombs. Most of the rubbish will be destroyed. The rest will be buried under lava and ash so deep it may never be found."

"Very well," said Alpha's master. "Now, finish off and report back to base. It is time to dump your next lot of rubbish."

"Understood," said Alpha. "We will report shortly."

"So, that's what these time-travelling robots are up to," Tori whispered. "In the year 3000, we have run out of room for waste disposal. They're using a disaster in the past to get rid of it instead!"

"Polluting history with future rubbish? That's horrible," said Ana. "But what about the old rockets and time ships in the ocean? They won't be affected in the water."

"Yes, they will," said Tori. "When it erupts, Vesuvius will send blasts of ultra-hot air down its slopes at 400 kilometres an hour; when that strikes the sea, the ocean will boil for miles around in a massive explosion that will destroy the old vehicles."

"But one of them exploded early by mistake," Rocco realised.

"Yes," said Tori. "By smashing the slaver's ship, it actually worked out well for us – but it might have caused a disaster. And the pollution it has released could hurt many animals in the sea."

Her satellite dish was spinning faster and faster. "In any case, messing about with time like this is dangerous! It's against the law! It makes me cross!"

"Keep your voice down, Tori," Ana urged her.

But it was too late.

"Intruders detected behind rock," said Alpha. "Zap them, Beta. Destroy them!"

7 Taking out the trash

From the top of the slope, Beta aimed its blaster at the boulder hiding Tori, Rocco and Ana. The three friends clung together in fear.

But then, with a hissing *WHOOSH*, a massive pink canister flew into view above the hilltop.

"It's a trash tin!" Rocco realised.

Alpha glared up at the floating container. "Someone must have found the trash tin remote control."

Beta nodded its blue, square head. "Level 3 alert! They may use it against ussssssssss ..."

Suddenly, both trash-bots staggered about as if pulled by some invisible force. Then, with an electronic cry, they flew backwards through the air as they were sucked up inside the trash tin!

Ana cheered. "That was amazing!"

"But what made it happen?" asked Tori.

"*I* did!" Ifan ran into sight at the top of the hill, waving a remote control. "I woke up in the time pod and saw those trash-bots climbing out of the big hole. I heard them threaten you, so I knew you were in trouble."

"But how did you find the remote for the trash tins?" asked Rocco.

"I didn't," said Ifan with a smile. "*She* did …"

Rocco and Ana rushed up the slope to the villa – and saw a familiar woman in a blue jumpsuit behind Ifan.

"Camilla from the market square!" cried Ana. "I thought you were selling your stuff at your stall. What are you doing here?"

"I went to the pit, looking for more junk," Camilla explained. "But I ran into some escaped slaves. They had been resting at the old villa before moving on to the north. They said that if I kept quiet about seeing them, they'd give me some of the strange treasure they'd found there. I wouldn't have told anyone anyway, but I was happy to accept their gift!"

"Camilla came here looking for *more* treasure and showed me what she'd got from upstairs. It was stuff that belonged to the trash-bots!" Ifan said happily. "An oil can, spare nuts and bolts – and this controller. It's marked 'TT'. 'TT' for Trash Tins!"

"A remote control!" cheered Tori. "That's how the trash-bots controlled them."

"See?" Ana grinned. "The villa's top floor really *is* the trash-bots' time ship in disguise!"

"I don't know what you're talking about, but your silver outfit is amazing," Camilla looked admiringly at Tori. "Did you find that here?"

"No," said Rocco. "She found it in another pit further round the coast, that-a-way." He pointed away from Oplontis. "Go now and you'll get the best stuff before anyone else."

"Really? Thanks for the tip! Bye!" Camilla sprinted off.

"Well done, Rocco," said Ana. "When the volcano does blow, she'll be safely out of the area."

"Let's hope the people Marcus captured got away, too," said Ifan. "Come on – let's use the trash-bots' time radio."

"NEVER!" The trash tin's lid broke open, and the trash-bots burst out from inside. They fired their laser guns. Tori and the children dived for cover behind statues and furniture as the deadly rays scorched the air and the two trash-bots ran inside the villa.

Ifan peeped out of his hiding place. "The trash-bots were too strong to stay trapped for long."

"They are heading for their time ship!" said Tori. "It will take a few minutes to warm up their engines. Then, they'll leave!"

"I have an idea," said Ifan. He passed the trash tins' remote control to Ana. "Quickly, use this to steer the trash tins over to the pit."

"And suck up all the rubbish?" Rocco smiled. "Good idea!"

"What are you going to do?" asked Ana.

Ifan ran to the hole to look at the blue magna-drag with its enormous magnets. "If we can get the magna-drag out, we can set it to maximum power."

"Maximum power?" Tori looked shocked. "That means the magna-drag will magnetise anything metal in the area and drag it here."

"Starting with the trash-bots' time ship, I hope!" said Ifan.

"It won't stop there," said Tori. "As the power builds, the trash tins, the old wrecks, everything – even the time pod – will be pulled together in a massive magnetic tangle."

"That's right! And the trash-bots' ship will be right at the centre," said Ifan excitedly. "The trash-bots will still be able to leave this time – but, because everything is stuck together, they'll take their rubbish with them!"

"You mean, if we fill the trash tins with all the plastic and fabric and non-magnetic junk, they'll take that stuff away, too!" said Ana. "Brilliant."

"I will switch on my anti-magnetic shield and help you, Ifan," said Tori. "But first we'll need to use the mega-digger to get the magna-drag out, and I'd better activate the time pod's brakes so it isn't pulled into the magna-drag, too."

"Come on, Ana," said Rocco.

Luckily, the trash tins were easy to control with the remote. Ana and Rocco steered all four of them from the villa to the pit.

"Now, we must set them to SUCK mode," said Ana.

Like hungry animals swallowing food, the trash tins gulped down all the rubbish. Their metal bodies began to bulge as they kept sucking up the debris until nothing was left.

"That's everything!" Ana beamed. "Come on, let's steer them back to the villa."

The closer they got to the villa, the faster the trash tins travelled. They were being magnetically pulled to the magna-drag. Rocco had to pull hard on the remote to stop them going out of control.

Outside the villa, the magna-drag was starting to shake. The top floor of the villa shook and began to shimmer.

"The trash-bots' ship is being pulled towards you," Ana shouted. "Get out of there!"

"Shelter in the time pod!" Rocco added.

Ifan and Tori hurried to the time pod and opened the door. Rocco and Ana joined them as they piled inside.

"Look, the trash-bots' ship is changing shape," said Tori. "The disguise isn't working any more. It's really ... a *coach*!"

Sure enough, the vehicle looked exactly like a coach from the year 3000! Two words were written on the side of it:

TIMELY TRIPS

"Timely Trips!" Tori shook in alarm. "They are the biggest rivals of Time Tours. Our worst competition! Why on Earth are they dumping rubbish in the past?"

The Timely Trips coach blasted its engines but could not escape being dragged towards the magna-drag. That made the magnetic pull even *more* powerful. Huge, dripping-wet, metal wrecks came tumbling across the landscape, drawn to the mass of metal.

"It's even dragged the old travel machines off the seabed!" said Ana.

BANG! SMASH! The wrecks kept crashing in, two or three at a time. The battered coach was completely boxed in by mangled metal wrecks! Finally, even the time pod was dragged in by the mega-magnetic pull.

Ifan breathed a sigh of relief. "I guess we got all the trash."

"And just in time," said Tori as the ground shook with sudden force. They watched as, in the distance, smoke and fire and rock burst from the top of Mount Vesuvius. It was an awesome, terrifying display of power.

Ana knew with a heavy heart that Pompeii and Oplontis would be buried beneath metres of ash and lava. They couldn't change that. It was a part of history – and was something she would never, ever forget.

At the centre of the magnetic mass, the Timely Trips coach started humming with more power than ever.

"The trash-bots have boosted their engines," yelled Ifan. "They're going to take off – dragging the magna-drag and all this metal waste with them."

"Including us!" squeaked Tori. "The time pod is now part of the magnetic mass. Wherever the trash-bots go – we will go, too!"

"They'll be going to meet their master," said Ana. "Whoever they are – we must stop them!"

As lava surged towards them, the coach, the magna-drag, the wrecks, the trash tins and the time pod all disappeared.

The children and Tori were back travelling through the mysterious flow of time ... ready for their next incredible adventure!

Chat about the book

1 Why was Camilla mistaken for a time traveller?

2 Go to page 25. Ana was wary of the stranger at the villa. What does 'wary' mean?

3 Read page 48. Why were Ana's eyes 'shining with excitement'?

4 Go to page 10. What do we learn about life on Earth in the year 3000?

5 Read page 32. How do Rocco, Ifan and Ana feel as the ship sets off?

6 Look at page 5. Why has the author ended with, 'If it isn't, who knows if we will ever get back home …?'

7 'Volcano of Fear' is about time travellers polluting history with future rubbish. Why do you think the author wanted to tell this story?

8 Is 'TIME TOURS – VOLCANO OF FEAR' a good title? Can you think of a different title the author might have used?